What Night Do the Angels Wander?

Phoebe Stone

What Night Do the Angels Wander?

Little, Brown and Company
Boston   New York   Toronto   London

What night do the angels wander the woods,
tossing fruits and acorns and seed
for the hungry rabbits and squirrels and birds
that come to the woods to feed?

And when do the angels skip and dance
in a crystal globe of light?
Around and around the lantern moon
they dance the wintry night.

And when do the angels stitch and sew
a great white quilt made of soft white snow?
They lift it high and they lift it low,
and snow gently covers the ground below.

What night do the angels wake the children
when the snow is fluffy and deep
and bring them to ride the silken swans
that float on the lake of sleep?

And when do the angels trim their tree
with clouds and mist and moon?
When do they sprinkle their tree with stars
from a gleaming silver spoon?

What night do the angels play their harps
in a delicate whispering key,
calling the elk, the deer, and the fawn
to circle the Christmas tree?

And they call to children around the world
to pass the candle along.
The light that burns is the spirit of love
that lives in the Christmas song.

What night do the angels sing and chant
as they roll out cookies and tarts?
And as they sing, we hear their song
deep in our sleeping hearts.

And when do the angels tip a bowl
of warm and glowing light
that cascades the earth with peace and joy
and breathes in the wind all night?

When do the angels fan the snow
so it rushes like wings from above?
And as they fan, it stirs our hearts
to give to those we love.

When do the angels with roses and wreaths
flutter and dip and fly?

When do they circle and spin and skate
on a midnight pond of sky?

What night is the angels' choir
with trumpets and strings and voice?

It's Christmas Eve! It's Christmas Eve!
When heaven and earth rejoice!

To my mother and father, Ruth and Walter Stone, and
my sisters, Abigail and Marcia, for all the beautiful
Christmases we shared many years ago

First Edition

Library of Congress Cataloging-in-Publication Data

Stone, Phoebe.
    What night do the angels wander? / Phoebe Stone. — 1st ed.
        p.   cm.
    Summary: Rhyming text describes the one night of the year when
    the angels come together to celebrate with the children and animals
    of the earth.
    ISBN 0-316-81439-3
    [1. Angels — Fiction.   2. Christmas — Fiction.   3. Stories in
    rhyme.]   I. Title.
PZ8.3.S872Wh   1998
[E] — dc21   97-10178

10 9 8 7 6 5 4 3 2 1

SC

Published simultaneously in Canada by Little, Brown & Company (Canada) Limited

Printed in Hong Kong

The illustrations for this book were done in pastels. The text was set in Stone Serif, and
the calligraphy for the display type was created by Judythe Sieck.